MAGMA

MAGMA

A Novel

THÓRA HJÖRLEIFSDÓTTIR

Translated from the Icelandic by
Meg Matich

Black Cat
New York

FIRST EDITION

Published simultaneously in Canada
Printed in the United States of America

Originally published in Icelandic in 2019 as *Kvika*
by Forlagid Agency, Reykjavik.

This book was set in 11-pt. Berling LT
by Alpha Composition & Design of Pittsfield, NH
The book was designed by Norman Tuttle
at Alpha Design & Composition

First Grove Atlantic paperback edition: July 2021

Library of Congress Cataloging-in-Publication data available for this title.

ISBN 978-0-8021-5739-3
eISBN 978-0-8021-5740-9

Black Cat
an imprint of Grove Atlantic
154 West 14th Street
New York, NY 10011

Distributed by Publishers Group West

groveatlantic.com

21 22 23 24   10 9 8 7 6 5 4 3 2 1

This account is fiction, populated by characters who speak to the realities that women have long lived in silence.

Shame and isolation thrive in that silence. If it isn't broken, this story will continue to repeat itself.

I dedicate this book to those who have spoken out.

MAGMA

Reykjavik 2007

Chlamydia

I didn't know it would be such a big deal; it's not like it's incurable. Nobody's going to die. We'll take antibiotics and then, ten days later, it'll be gone. But now he thinks I'm a total slut. And I must be, since I've infected people. But I think he's being unfair. It shouldn't matter this much. He acts like I've rejected him because I've been with other men. We weren't together when I went to Central America; we'd gone on one date and I hadn't even slept with him. I was traveling alone, so I slept around because I had nothing better to do and I needed to fill in the gaps. I didn't know that something would grow between us; in fact, I thought it'd never happen, but I became more and more taken with him as I traveled. He sent me near-constant emails and he was always ready to talk when I went to internet cafés. We just started to connect. When I came home, we clicked; I fell head over heels. He's beautiful and smart—I don't know how many books he owns, hundreds at least, and he has this crazy DVD collection.

But the chlamydia kept eating at him. He wouldn't stop interrogating me about the other boys. I held back at first. I only told him about one guy, a Norwegian in Cuba, and then I added the next one to the list—followed by the third, the fourth, the fifth, fuck, I can't be expected to remember everything. I tried to explain that my memory isn't really that great, but he thinks I'm lying. We were gliding on a smooth current, and now he wants nothing to do with me.

Bachelors I

He's moved into a basement apartment in Vestur-bær on the west side of town with a friend who is the very embodiment of a tragic bachelor. His roommate can't even take care of himself—he's at least thirty, but he hasn't learned how to wash his clothes properly. He just leaves his wet clothes in the machine until they dry. The place is a cesspool. Their towels are all sour, and the smell gets pretty pungent when you dry off. And his roommate doesn't cook, either. On a good day, he might boil a hot dog, but he seems to live on bodega burgers, chocolate chip cookies, and Diet Coke. He's crazy about Diet Coke; in the morning, he shuffles out of his room in a sloppy navy bathrobe and the first thing he does is swig flat Coke from the bottle. I don't understand how he can live with this guy. But it's nice to be able to hang out by ourselves. We aren't together, but I'm with him all the time.

Vegetarians

I think it's awesome that he's a vegetarian, too; none of my friends are, and the girls are always teasing me about it. But we've banded together in our meat-free lifestyle—plus, he's a great vegetarian cook, so I'm learning a lot. I've started to eat a much more balanced diet. I've graduated from grilled cheese and fries. He thinks it's offensive when people invite him to dinner and then offer him meat—and all his girlfriends have been vegetarians. He thinks girls who eat meat are repulsive.

The Ex I

He still loves his ex-girlfriend, and they're still close friends. She's elegant and clever. She was at the top of her class in classics in school, they both know Latin, and they're both well-read; they toss Derrida quotes around like it's nothing. The other day, he asked me to meet him at a coffeehouse, so it was more than a little strange that he was sitting with her when I arrived. I felt humiliated, and I wanted to leave, to turn around and walk straight out, to disappear, but they'd already spotted me and I had to sit with them. It was one of the most uncomfortable afternoons of my life. I was stressed, sweating like a pig, and I got this weird tremor. They were so relaxed together, and so much smarter than me. They talked about movies I hadn't seen, and they went on and on about things I hadn't ever thought about. The Ex tried to bring me into the conversation by explaining, among other things, what a *strawberry milkshake* was—it's when a man cums on a woman's face and punches her in the nose, giving her a nosebleed. *Snowballing*, she went on, is when a man cums in a woman's mouth and she spits it into his mouth. He's told me about sex with her—how nice it was, how talented she is at blow jobs. I'm pretty bad at them; I just gag.

The Bike

He asked me to meet him at the bar one night, but I was home in the suburbs in Grafarvogur with my mom and dad, and I didn't feel like it. I didn't say it like that; I just said I was going to be with my little sister, but he got moody and weird. We were pretty much always together, so it felt like we'd become dependent on each other. That night, I noticed I couldn't stand to sleep alone anymore; I was cold and I missed him. It was hard to fall asleep, I felt off, and I regretted not going out to meet him, but I felt a little guilty, too, for how little I'd seen my parents in the past few weeks. I tossed and turned because I couldn't stop replaying the phone call in my head. I wanted to meet him, to check on him. Since I couldn't sleep, I decided that I'd hop into my mom's car and head to Vesturbær—I was going to surprise him, sneak into his bed, and wake up with him.

The front door to his place is always unlocked, so I showed myself in. In the entryway, I saw his shoes, alongside a pair of expensive heels from Kron. Sexy heels. I knew his roommate wouldn't have brought home the type of girl who'd own these shoes. I figured that she'd be in the bed I'd gone there to slip into, and I didn't need to go into the room to confirm it. I knew it. I knew in my gut that I hadn't been enough. It's obvious. I really thought we were going to be together—I'm a fucking idiot. Another woman always comes along.

I tiptoed into the bathroom and grabbed my toothbrush, my toiletries, my birth control. He'd wake up with this new girl and it'd be as if I'd never been there. My bike was outside the apartment, and I wheeled it over to the car. I was going to disappear from his life with all my stuff, and he wouldn't even notice. The bike was really heavy, and it took me a while to figure out how to angle the wheel so that it fit into the trunk. I could never lift that bike by myself, but that night, I hardly felt a thing as I flung it over my shoulder and forced it into the car in a rush of adrenaline. I drove for a few minutes, parked the car by the ocean at a stretch of shore called Ægissíða, and howled with tears until there were no tears left, and then, and only then, did I trust myself to drive back to Grafarvogur. Everybody was still asleep. I snuck into my room and never let on that I'd gone out during the night.

I won't speak to him again. I should've known that I'd never be good enough for him. If I'd just gone to the bar when he asked me, maybe this wouldn't have happened. The girl with the great shoes is probably a vegetarian, I don't want to know who she is, fucking slut.

Willpower I

He called, left a message, but I was a Teflon woman—
everything slid off me.

Willpower II

For about fifteen minutes.

Graduation Party

He invited me to his cousin's graduation party. I was more than a little excited. This definitely meant that he wanted to be my boyfriend soon. You don't just take your fuckbuddy to your cousin's grad party. His younger cousin had passed all her exams, which took everyone by surprise; her mother sprang into action, planning the entire gathering in less than a day. The party was in Selfoss, an hour drive for us, but it's where his family lives. I borrowed my mom's car, and as we drove past the lava fields at Hellisheiði, he told me that all his cousins on his mother's side had competed in the Miss Southern Iceland pageant—it'd practically become a sport in his family. He's good-looking, too, but he isn't into these girls who cake on makeup for the county fair. I'm probably the first girl his cousin will meet who still has hair on her pussy.

I felt like a weed among the roses at the party; he didn't introduce me to anyone, and he didn't speak to anyone. He'd brought a book, which he read in a bedroom while his aunts and his mom sized me up in the living room. He hates chitchatting at these gatherings, it's pointless, he says, so he always packs something to read. He says that parties give him time to enrich his internal life, to learn in the midst of mediocrity. He's had enough of talking about the weather and how school is going.

After a while, his mom settled on introducing me as "a friend of her son." Then his grandmother, who had sunk into a deep recliner in the living room, called out, "You know he has kids?" as she nibbled creamy cake from a tiny fork.

The aunts waited for the penny to drop. "Yes, I know about that," I answered, holding my voice steady.

His grandmother continued: "I don't think he'll ever finish university. He really loves to read." She let out a raspy laugh as she bent forward in the recliner, her plate seeming to refill itself with her daughter's endless pastries.

His Children

He has very little contact with his children, and I've never met them. He had a daughter with a friend from high school when they were only seventeen. They were never together, and he put no effort into forming a relationship; he found her parents trying. They seemed to hate him as much as they loved their grandchild. He was a really promising soccer player at the time, and the summer his daughter was born, he rushed from match to match and missed the whole third trimester, including the birth. He had a very difficult time after the baby was born because nobody had put him down as the father, and when Baby Mama #1 finally added his name to the certificate, he was charged half a year of back child support, the first six months of his daughter's life. He says that even though she's flaky, the mother is a good person; she settled down in Selfoss and has a husband and more kids.

His other baby mama is apparently a complete psycho. She never lets him see their boy. She's still upset because he asked her to have an abortion when she told him she was pregnant. He tried to visit her after the baby was born, but she berated him and badgered him about the right way to hold a baby. Once, in a snowstorm in January, she threw him out in his socks and refused to give his shoes back. All that drama really took a toll on him; it's why he and His Clever Ex aren't together anymore, even if they're friends. She couldn't deal with the whole baby situation. I still haven't told my parents about his kids. He asked me not to mention it, at least not right away.

Hygiene

When I shower at his place, he always wants to get in with me. We've showered together so often that he seems quite hurt if I say I'd like to shower alone. The shower is really tight with two people, especially when I wash my hair, but he thinks it's cozy, and I want to make him happy. Sometimes when we shower, he asks if he can pee on me. Urine feels strange when it runs down your body; it's colder than the water, and the smell that cooks in the heat and steam isn't especially pleasant. He usually wants to piss on my back. But sometimes he wants me to rest on my knees while he pees over my head. Once, he peed in my mouth. I didn't like that. But I don't mind the other times as much, as I'm already in the shower and can rinse it right off.

Mom

One morning, we woke up to the shrill ring of his cell. "It's just Mom," he said dismissively, letting it ring until she hung up. But she called again and again, and he rolled his eyes, switched it to silent, and rolled back over in bed.

"Aren't you going to answer?" I asked, watching the green light of his cell phone continue to blink. He mumbled something as he fell back to sleep. But I was wide-awake, listening to the buzzing of her calls until well past noon.

His mom always does his laundry for him. She comes all the way from Selfoss to drop off his clean clothes, drives home with a dirty load. She's obsessed with cleaning. He says that he's hardly ever sat down to a meal without her coming running with a cloth to scrub a spot or a spill or something. She lives with her new husband in a big house. Everything is impeccable. The furniture perfectly matches the drapes, the figurines. She believes that work dignifies and enriches the soul, and she doesn't understand why he's so focused on education. But he's been at the university for eight years and he's halfway to a heap of degrees.

He says that people from the South don't see the point of educating themselves, since they can start working at the slaughterhouse straight out of tenth grade and bring in more bread than most academics with a liberal arts education ever will. I think it's terrible that he's so misunderstood by his own family, but I also think it's a shame that he doesn't answer his mom when she's calling so urgently.

Ghosts of the Past

Before I met him, I was promiscuous. I didn't think that sex was a big deal. I thought it was exciting. So I slept around—with all kinds of guys. But I really regret it now because when we go downtown and a boy says hi to me and then walks out of earshot, he snaps, "Did you sleep with that one, too?" I usually answer yes.

When I was eighteen, I got my first and only boyfriend. He seemed wonderful up until my birthday, when he fucked another girl. That marked the beginning of a long period when we couldn't bring ourselves to break up, and we flushed whatever good there was left right down the toilet. After that, I started sleeping around, and I acted like a complete jerk more often than not—like the time I had sex with a lanky artsy guy at the party of another friend who had a huge crush on me. Or when I crashed in my friend's tiny apartment on her cramped couch and brought home some guy I'd known in high school. But I didn't think any of it was really important. Just two pieces of meat kneading each other, trying to find an orgasm that would make them forget, if only for a fleeting second, how empty their lives are.

He takes it personally. "What does that say about me?" he asks. "All these guys are so fucking ugly, and you keep adding more and more to the list." Sometimes he gets so worked up he says, "An attractive man like me can't be with a girl who's slept with so many creeps."

The Ex II

He always speaks so fondly of his Ex. They meet up pretty often, and I'm really uncomfortable with it, but I'm not exactly in a position to interfere. I think she's still into him. He told me recently that they'd been hanging out, watching a movie, and they'd kissed, and he could have slept with her if he'd wanted, but he didn't because he knew it would hurt me. It's all so disheartening—the way he talks about her so brightly, with such warmth in his voice, and how he's always comparing me to her. He's already told her everything, including how I'd given him chlamydia, but he guards all her secrets fiercely. I think he still feels bad about the way their relationship ended, back when she was still in high school. After her family found out that he had two kids, they didn't want her to have anything to do with him, and they tried to come between them. Complete fucking Romeo and Juliet bullshit. Sometimes I try to get him to trash her—but it's like he thinks she's some sort of saint, and he'll concede only that she's had her problems, she's sensitive, and she's never given him an STI.

Girlfriends

My girlfriends aren't exactly thrilled with him. They've met him a few times, but it's always ended badly. When he ran into Emma at Bakkus, this dive bar downtown, he punched her in the kidney to show her how effective it was as a self-defense move. She said that she had to lie on the floor until it stopped hurting. When he came home late that night, he was inconsolable. It was supposed to be a joke; he hadn't realized that she would double over like that. He didn't mean to hurt her.

Another night, when he bumped into Sigrún at Sirkus, he ended up making her cry. She sent me a text that night, saying she never wanted to see him again and she missed me. But she didn't tell me what happened between them. I felt really guilty. I've been with him so much lately that I've completely ignored my own friends. But there are so many things I can't tell them. If you talk about what happens within a relationship, everything gets tangled, and it's easy for an outsider to judge—I don't want them to write him off completely. They don't know what it's like to be as in love as I am now.

Butthole

We were watching a film, cuddled up on the couch, when he first asked if he could—maybe, possibly, someday—fuck me in the ass. I thought at first that he was joking. Nobody wants to do that. Not really. I know that one of my friends did it, and she said it was disgusting. And I've heard that it's pretty dangerous. Sigrún's mom is a nurse, and she's told her horror stories about teenage girls who come into the emergency room with torn sphincters because of rough anal. They have to wear diapers for the rest of their lives because they have no control over their bowel movements; the shit just spills out. I understand that gay men make do with their situation by penetrating each other, but straight men with healthy women in their beds—women who have vaginas, mouths, and hands—should really count their blessings.

Love

I love him, but I'm not going to tell him, not yet anyway. I don't believe he loves me back, but we're getting there. And I don't care. It's enough when he touches me, wraps his arms around me, fucks me. When he looks at me with his gray eyes, a wave of bliss surges over me, and he's given me orgasms that make my toes tingle. Sometimes you don't have to use words to voice every little thing. I can tell that he cares about me, too; I'm not going to scare him off by insisting. It'd be too pushy to tell him that I love him now. That sort of statement demands a reaction, and I don't want a reaction, I just want him as he is, right now. Everything is empty and pointless compared with him. I feel like I could leave my self behind just to love this man.

The Suburbs

We went to dinner at my parents' house. I was so proud to introduce them to the mysterious man I've been spending all my time with. They'd even baked vegetarian lasagna for us. But I was caught off guard by how small and strange he acted in front of my parents. He diverted his gaze, looking down at his shoes when he shook their hands, and the whole time, he never once looked them in the eyes. My sister gaped at him in astonishment when he took a book out in the middle of dinner. It was very strange. But as soon as he picked up on it, he put the book down. My mom and dad were sociable and tried to engage with him, asking him about his studies at university, his family, and things like that, but he responded by staring at his plate and mumbling inaudibly. I still haven't mentioned his kids to them.

Privilege

I don't have a real frame of reference for understanding him. My life's been so comfortable. I have parents who love me, support me, and help me whenever I need it. He's never had it as good as I have. Even though his mother does everything she can to help him now, it was a very different story when he was little. His real dad was a Norwegian soldier his mother met when she was working in Oslo. They were married for a little while, but they divorced when he was still a kid. His mom moved back to Selfoss, where she struggled with being poor, working two jobs to make ends meet. He went to stay with his father one summer, and his dad refused to give him back. He made him call his mom and tell her—in Norwegian—that he wanted to live with him. His dad convinced his mom that her child was better off in Norway, as he had a good salary from the military and a boy needed his father more than his mother in order to become a man. For years, he was at the mercy of a violent drunk, and the only moments of relief were when his father had girlfriends who he beat even more. A distraction. In the end, Child Protective Services got involved when one of his father's exes reported him. So he was sent back home to his mom. They've never talked about what happened, but his mom tries to be good to him, maybe as a way of compensating for what happened to him as a kid. But it's like he's angrier with her than he is with his dad.

That's why he was so weird when he met my parents; he's not used to being around normal people, a typical family like us. I'm going to help him. I've always had it so good that it's easy enough for me to shoulder a little of the pain he's carried for so long. I'll make it better.

The Game I

One night, we went out with one of his childhood friends for drinks downtown at Kaffibarinn. I got the impression that his friend was a very lonely guy. He'd never had a girlfriend, and it seemed like he couldn't speak to women without making some sort of horrible blunder. He had recently gotten into a book called *The Game* about pickup artists who use a variety of tricks and techniques to bait women into hooking up. In the book, men are encouraged to toy with women's insecurities. If the player is interested in a woman and she's got a friend, for example, he's supposed to shower her friend with praise and give the target the cold shoulder.

His childhood friend invites him out all the time to act as wingman because it can help, apparently, to have an attractive friend with you. This evening, I was going with them, to help his friend meet girls, and I thought it would show what a good girlfriend I'd make.

I met a girl at the bar and chatted with her a bit. She'd lost her friends, and I thought it was a golden opportunity to invite her to join us, so I introduced her to the boys. We were all standing around a high table, joking about the bright summer nights, and they seemed to hit it off. The friend had finally gotten his chance. But then he said out of nowhere, "Lilja thinks you're ugly, but I don't think that at all."

The girl looked at me in bewilderment, and embarrassed, I mumbled, "I never said that. I think you're awesome."

But she disappeared into the crowd before I could get another word in. The friend said he didn't understand why she was being so dramatic. She must be crazy.

As we walked home, just the two of us, I asked if his friend was on the spectrum. He shrugged his shoulders and said that that's just the game.

The Game II

The next weekend, the boys went out again. I was invited along, but I had zero interest in hanging out with his childhood friend and taking part in that bullshit again. He told me that they'd just started to walk up the hill on Bankastræti when they met two good-looking girls. He felt bad for his friend because he had absolutely no luck with women, and at that moment, he realized that the time for talk was over. It was time for action.

The girls on Bankastræti were both nineteen, and one of them was a vegetarian. They chatted, and before he knew it, she'd invited him back to her place. They left his friend and the other girl behind and hopped into a taxi, on their way to the suburbs. They went in her hot tub, where she gave him a hand job, and later they had sex. The morning after, he took the bus home to Vesturbær, where I'd stayed all night, and told me about that night's game. He thought it was impressive that he didn't even need to go into a bar to pick up a girl; he was so attractive, he could do it on the way there. I started to cry, but in a way it was my own fault. If I'd have gone with them, this never would've happened. He was just trying to help his friend.

Prevention I

In Cuba, I smoked filterless cigarettes called Flor de Aroma. They're the best cigarettes I think I've ever smoked, hand-rolled in the region. They smell of tobacco flowers. They weren't as strong as cigars, but they were still intense. I smoked up all of them right after I left the tropics.

He thinks smoking is ridiculous. Only idiots smoke, he says. I've really cut down on my smoking, and now I only do it when I'm out or if I'm at a café. But after I've smoked, he sniffs me, frowns, refuses to kiss me. He says that I stink. The other day, he took it to the next level—he wants me to quit smoking, and for every cigarette I smoke from now on, he's going to fuck eight women. I don't want him to sleep with more girls. He should only be with me. I'll never smoke again.

Non Grata

He'll never be my boyfriend. I don't understand why I'm always with him. When we run into people he knows, he doesn't introduce me, he talks to them as if I'm not there. He's very private. He would be uncomfortable if everyone knew everything about him, but sometimes I feel like I'm disappearing. Especially when he doesn't come back to his apartment, even though he knows I sleep there most nights. It doesn't happen often, but it does happen. The other day I stayed up all night watching DVDs, waiting for him to come home from the bar. He was surprised that I was still awake in his living room when he finally came home in the morning. He'd been with some redhead. She lives with

her boyfriend, so they fucked on the old, crusty couch
in the study hall at the university. I know that I have
to end things, but I can't tear myself away from him.
If I were better, then I'd be enough.

Oral Sex

I've been working on my blow jobs. It's not going very well. I always gag, sometimes loudly, and throw up in my mouth. But now I've started to swallow the puke and the bile and keep going instead of giving up right away, like I always did before. When I blow him, tears run down my cheeks, but I'm not crying, it's just a reflex. I'm always surprised by how long it takes—I'm at it for half an hour or something before he cums, but in porn, it only takes about two minutes. Maybe I'm doing something wrong. But sometimes I can't keep going, and it's always right before he ejaculates, and then he gets pissed off and looks at my face, which is usually covered in tears, and says, "Wow, is being with me really that good?"

Plato's Moon Child

It's incredible to me that this big, strong man can also seem just like a fragile little boy. When we sleep together at night, he wraps himself around me, so peaceful and beautiful. We lie heavily against each other the entire night. Our bodies are two pieces of a puzzle. When we lie together, I feel like I'm finally complete. There's neither too much nor too little; only a simple precision, just as it should be. Some mornings, when I wake up, he's so hungry for me that he's already pushed himself inside me. It's almost automatic how he just slips in. Then he's so gentle that I feel a sting of gratitude.

Vanity I

I really don't own cosmetics; I've never been very good at dressing myself up. My makeup bag is so empty that when I unzip it, I expect moths to fly out. But instead, old mascara, half-empty powder, lipstick, and a Swiss Army knife clink around inside the bag. I bought the knife right before I traveled to Central America. I mainly used it to open beer, but I once used it to slice a mango on a beach on the way south, in Mexico.

It's so wonderful how he likes me exactly as I am. He gets irritated, seems even hurt, if I put on makeup, and he asks accusingly, "Who are you doing that for?" I don't understand why he gets so jealous; I would never want to be with anyone else. He's so ethical, unlike anyone I've ever met. He just doesn't want me to poison him with additives and preservatives. I don't need to wear lipstick for him; he thinks my bare lips are perfectly kissable.

Internet Friends I

He's always chatting on the internet. Sometimes it's like he disappears into his laptop. When he's off in his digital world, I can't reach him. We first became friends on the internet. We got wrapped up in each other. When I was in Central America, I was often lonely, and the time difference didn't seem to matter: he was always online when I needed somebody to talk to. Now we're on the same continent, in the same country, in the same home, and he's more distant than ever. He's still on the computer, grinning, sniggering over some bit of cleverness while I'm hanging out, waiting for him to turn his attention to me.

The other day, when I was washing up after dinner, he sat down in the living room with his computer.

"I thought we were going to watch a movie," I said as I dried my hands on a dirty kitchen towel, but he didn't reply. I made a few attempts to reach him, to lure him to me, to no avail. I went into his room, closed myself in, and half hoped he would chase me, but he never came. I took off my pants, lay in his bed, and masturbated. Serves him right, I thought, his loss. Still, it would've been even better if he'd walked in on me and realized that there was a person of flesh and blood in his apartment who wanted him here, now.

Bachelors II

I feel so sorry for his roommate. He recently had a birthday, and his family gave him a vacuum cleaner as some sort of half-serious joke. Three weeks later, it's still in the box in the hallway. His roommate has continued to wear nothing but his perpetual bathrobe, and he's continued to eat cheap burgers from the corner shop. When he doesn't want a warm meal, he eats stuffed Oreos and slugs Diet Coke. I've never met such a Coke nut.

Nobody ever visits his roommate. If I lived alone, I'd always invite people to parties and dinner. He must be very lonely. A few days ago the strangeness of their living situation really hit me. The roommate had locked himself in his room and was listening to

Damien Rice, the same CD, the volume cranked up, over and over and over and over. We were in the front room watching a film when we heard the music from his room, so we started laughing about the sad Saturday night sing-along alone in his room. By the time we went to bed, he'd turned it down a little. The same song on repeat, the singer meowing, "*Cold, cold, water surrounds me now . . .*"

As the night wore on, the music continued, and I began to feel really perturbed. Maybe he'd offed himself and we were just giggling on the other side of the wall. I asked him if he'd go and check on his roommate, to see if something was wrong. But he was tired, and he said, "No, no, he'll be fine." In the morning, we were sitting in the kitchen and eating our cereal when his roommate stepped out of his room, unkempt and ashen. He mumbled some sort of greeting, tightened the belt of his robe, grabbed a half-empty bottle of Diet Coke, retreated to his room, and put Damien Rice back on.

The Ex III

One evening, when we'd slipped into bed, his Ex-Girlfriend called him. The conversation was brief, and when he hung up, he leaped out of bed. "There's a midnight launch at the bookstore, the seventh Harry Potter book is coming out," he gasped.

"Why is your ex-girlfriend calling you about that? Can't we just buy the book in the morning?" I tried to hide how bitter I felt, as I didn't want to give him the pleasure of knowing I was jealous. He looked at me as he shoved his feet into his socks.

"She's just a friend. We read all the other books together. I'm just going to run and grab this last one." He pulled on his pants and ran out of the room.

The Ex IV

The next night, his Ex called him again. We were lying naked in bed, and he seemed surprised to see her name blinking on his screen so late at night. He answered, moving away so that I wouldn't hear what they were saying. He listened for a long time before quickly turning to look at me. Finally he said, "Ya, I knew about that," and hung up.

"What does she want now?" I asked, a deliberate frown crossing my face. He was flustered, evasive: "She said she'd heard a rumor about you . . . that you were raped and you blogged about it."

The wind was knocked out of me, like I'd been punched in the stomach. Then I erupted.

"That's such fucking bullshit. What business is it of hers? Why didn't you say something? Why didn't you defend me? I deleted that entry a long time ago. Right after I wrote the damn thing. Do you think it's okay for her to shoot her mouth off like some vicious Mean Girl?" I started to wail, and he lay down beside me in bed, wrapping his arms around me.

"My ex has been through a lot; she's very sensitive. I don't know, maybe she's a little jealous. I mean, look who's in bed with me now."

"What's so fucking difficult for her? Just tell me, then we're even."

"I can't talk about her secrets. I can't break her trust. We hold each other's confidence. Trust me, she's damaged."

That night I cried myself to sleep—not because I pitied myself because of the rape, but because I knew he'd never watch over me half as well as he watches over her.

Ephemera

I was raped this weekend. I swear I wasn't trying to get with that guy, I didn't even like him, but that's how it goes. One way or another, we all lose our virginity somehow.

Deflowering

When I was seventeen, I moved to Denmark as an au pair. I lived with Louise, who was a good friend of my parents. Louise lived in a village with her family—a sailor who was often at sea, a three-year-old daughter, and a big dog. I went to a high school in town to work on my Danish and to have something to do during the day while the little girl was in preschool. It took me a long time to make friends with the kids in my class, because I refused to speak English with them.

In the end, I made friends with Anne, an unpopular girl who was obsessed with her ex and loved Linkin Park. She was fucking boring, but I had to start somewhere. Anne said we should go out together some evening. I was up for it, since the main reason I came to

Demark was to drink beer and smoke cigarettes. Anne and I met at my place one evening and shotgunned a few cheap beers. There wasn't really much of a bar scene in the village—one pub that we didn't want to go to, and one bar where other teenagers went to party. There, we bumped into an Icelandic boy and some of his friends. They all looked like small-time criminals, with bleached hair and ripped jeans, dripping with sickly sweet aftershaves. This boy was the first Icelander I'd seen in two months. I chatted with him for a long time—I think his name was Steinn or Steinar. We didn't have anything in common other than our language—no shared interests—but I was glad to be able to speak freely without feeling like I was stupid. His scummy companions kept buying us drinks, we did shots, and as the night wore on, Steinn Steinar asked if I wanted to do a line with him. I'd never tried anything like that, but I felt up for it in that moment, at that level of intoxication. We snorted something in the bathroom, he tried to kiss me, but I slipped out from under his arms and made a break for the dance floor. After that, there was only bass, noise, dance, touch, black, nothing.

The morning after, I woke up in my bed feeling like I'd been hit by a train. When I got up, the floor was covered in broken glass, but I rushed past it and made it to the bathroom just in time to throw up. I puked and puked, with short pauses to lie down on the living room sofa, where I sweated and shook under a blanket. When Louise got out of bed, she teased me, said I'd been pretty wasted when I came home. I'd slammed the front door so loud the house shook, and I'd knocked over a couple of plants on my way up to my room. She noticed that I was bruised. I had deep scratches on one of my thighs, like I'd fallen and skinned my whole right side on the pavement. My body was covered in small cuts and bruises. Louise kept asking me what happened at the bar, and finally I gave in and told her that I thought I'd been raped. I left out the part where I'd taken drugs, instead saying that Steinn Steinar must have slipped me something.

We went to the emergency clinic, where I was examined, and based on the injuries, there was no doubt I'd been raped. I'd never slept with anyone before, and now my vagina was covered in contusions, torn. It was a wound. I was grateful that I hardly remembered anything. It's still a blur—my head was hit or hit against something hard, and I saw Steinn Steinar wild against me in the bathroom, which was covered in graffiti. The nurse encouraged me to report the rape, but I didn't want to, I knew it was my own fault. I shouldn't have taken drugs. All I had to do was say "No, thanks," and it never would have happened, I wouldn't have lost my senses. My parents would feel really bad if they found out that I'd broken their trust, right when they'd let me move to a foreign country. It was bad enough that I had to call them and tell them about the rape.

At school on Monday, Anne came over to me and announced proudly that she'd gone home with one of Steinn's sleazy friends and he was her new boyfriend. Then she asked teasingly about what happened between Steinn Steinar and me. I'd completely disappeared! I told her that Steinn had slipped me something and raped me and I'd gone to the hospital the day after. When Anne heard that, she laughed sloppily and said, "That makes no sense. He couldn't have raped you. You were hitting on him so hard."

Academia

Starting university was tougher than I expected. I'd always been a good student, and I'd never been challenged really, but now I felt overwhelmed when it came to these new assignments. I was barely getting by, with really bad grades, and all my essays came back to me marked up, comments screaming in red ink.

Fortunately, he's been in university for a long time and knows how to do it all. He's so clever, and he weaves together these smart, scholarly texts out of nothing. Sometimes he writes essays for me when he has the time. I'm doing much better.

Internet Friends II

We're always together at his place. I've even started to hang out there when he isn't home. It's great because he lives so close to the university, and he knows where to find me. I know that he talks to other girls on the internet. Sometimes I spy on him and read over his shoulder to find out who he's talking to. He can't stand it. He's very private; he doesn't want me to use his computer unless he's with me. He sometimes talks to the red-haired girl he fucked, but he insists that they're just friends. I have male friends, and he says that I need to accept that he has female friends, too.

Prevention II

I went to the craft store on Skólavörðustígur and bought glass paint. For the past few weeks I've been collecting little jars that could make beautiful candleholders. I thought we could paint them together. It would be a nice change from watching films and having sex. I thought he would be excited about it, but he made a scene of plunking down into a chair at the kitchen table, where he sulked, taking one of the little jars in his big hands.

He wasn't dexterous enough to use the fine brushes I'd bought for the occasion. The paints ran and smudged together, and his jar became, in the end, a green-gray muddy color, as if a three-year-old child had been painting. He pushed the ugly jar away and heaved a sigh of resignation, washed his hands, and walked off with the computer folded under his arm. I stayed behind, painting jar after jar in gorgeous colors and shapes. If he takes one of his online girls home with him, maybe they'll notice these intricately painted tealights, and they'll have the decency to fuck off.

Limits I

He keeps asking me about anal sex. I just say that I don't understand why he wants it so much. Then he gets this dreamy look on his face and says he can't even describe how good it feels. So tight and unique—something totally different. In the end, I gave in.

It wasn't good or bad, just uncomfortable, and I was so stressed the entire time. I worried that his penis might be like a plunger and when he took it out of me, shit would just empty all over the bed. But that didn't happen. When he was finished, he was so euphoric that I couldn't do anything other than feel happy along with him. I want him to believe I'm the best in bed.

Limits II

He's started to do it regularly—ride me in the ass. Once, he went from there straight into my pussy. I asked him to stop, asked him if I could just get a washcloth. I pictured his penis, the little clots of fecal matter that clung to it as it slid into my vagina. It was like an extreme version of wiping in the wrong direction. But he was so horny and so hungry for me that he couldn't stop before he got off.

Birthday

I went to my friend Sigrún's birthday party. He didn't want to come along. "It's your friend's birthday, I don't see why I have to go." I'm not his girlfriend; I don't have any right to drag him to some girly party. I'm never invited on the rare occasion that he actually goes out with his friends. I only exist to him when it's just us two.

It was a pretty big party; Sigrún and Emma live together in an apartment building on the west side of town—and the party was a big hit. I had a couple of cocktails and was in a really good mood until I saw her. The Ex was in Sigrún's class in high school and she'd come with a few of her friends. She greeted me, and I responded as coldly as I could and then ignored her aggressively. The Ex wasn't there for very long, anyway; Sigrún and I are much closer than those two. I refilled my glass again and again, and the wine opened the floodgates. Tears, forcing themselves to the surface, uncontrollable. I closed myself in a bedroom and started to cry and cry and cry and cry. I couldn't stop, even though I knew I was acting like an idiot. A little while later, all the guests left, and I didn't know whether I was the reason or if they'd just gone downtown.

I stepped outside and met the girls, who were gathering up bottles and cans. I couldn't talk, couldn't explain anything. I could only say sorry and cry convulsively. I stayed with Emma, and she wrapped her arms around me until I wore myself out. Near morning, I crept out of bed. He would've lost it if I hadn't come back to his place, and I wanted to be sure that nobody else was in his bed.

Bad

I think I'm losing my mind. I've been so crazy that I haven't seen the writing on the wall. He's never going to be my boyfriend, especially if I act like this. But I can't control myself—I'm always crying, always sensitive, always horrible. The last time I gave him a blow job, I powered through it until he ejaculated, and then I ran to the bathroom and retched and vomited. I collapsed on the floor and lay there among the pubic hairs and piss stains and cried. I was ashamed for being so pathetic. I beat my head against the toilet, feeling like an animal that had locked its own cage.

I looked at my ugly face in the mirror and tried to wipe away the tears, calm the swelling. I fumbled for my makeup bag to freshen up. But instead, I fished out the red pocketknife, untucked a sharp blade, and cut a few scratches on the inside of my thigh. I don't know why. I'd never done anything like that before. But I watched the blood bead and run down my thigh toward my knee, and for a little while, I felt better. The cut let out the pressure in my head—I wasn't going to explode, I had stopped crying. Everything bad had been gathered together into this little scratch—just a normal wound. It served me right, felt right.

Equation

The very best thing for me would be to end it with him and to stop being such a psycho. But I can't stay away from him for very long. I can't lose him. I love him with every cell in my body and I would waste away without him. Whether I stay or go, I'll still be crazy. It all adds up to the same thing.

Vanity II

I've started cutting myself regularly. I always use the red pocketknife, making scratches on my forearms and thighs. I do it when I'm bad in bed or when I'm just bad. He thinks the scratches are disgusting; they're all over me, and when he sees them, he just shakes his head. "Why are the beautiful ones always crazy?"

I don't have an answer. I'm just damaged goods, but it made me happy that he called me beautiful.

Wedding

One of his childhood friends is going to get married in Selfoss, and he invited me to come with him. It's the first time that I'll meet any of his friends, apart from his roommate and his hopeless pickup artist pal. The ceremony was beautiful, everyone at the reception drunk on love. His friends thought I was really great, and one even said to him in astonishment, "Where have you been hiding this one?" We drank and danced, he twirled me in a circle on the dance floor and kissed me in front of everyone. He's usually so private; he never does anything like that.

As night approached, we took a bus with his friends back to Reykjavik. On the way, he kissed me and, for the first time, said that he loved me. He said it again and again, *I love you, I love you*. When we arrived in town, I was pretty tired and much too drunk, so I went straight to his place. He went to Kaffibarinn with his friends. I woke up alone the next morning. He came home around noon and jumped straight into the shower.

He loves me.

He loves me.

He loves me.

He loves me.

He loves me.

He loves me.

He loves me.

He loves me.

He loves me.

He loves me.

He loves me.

He loves me.

He loves me.

He loves me.

He loves me.

He loves me.

He loves me.

He loves me.

He loves me.

The Sticking Place

Even though everything is better now, I still feel like I'm unraveling. He loves me, finally, but I've lost my footing and I can't enjoy it. His girls get in the way. He sometimes talks to the red-haired girl on the internet and I think it's weird. But he says it's none of my business what he does on the internet, and she's only his friend.

I try to be good in bed, but when I get it wrong, I hurt myself in some way. Once, he was having anal sex with me and I started to cry. I was so ashamed for being such a baby that when he finished, I beat my head on the headboard with all my strength, leaving a huge bump. I'm covered in scratches. The other day he grabbed my forearm—there was a trickle of blood—and barked, "Stop this! You're just doing it for attention. It's all an act."

Maybe he was trying to snap me out of it, but I went back into the bathroom, locked myself in, and cut a few deep lines into my arm so that the blood poured all over the place. The scars will be nasty after this one.

Blue Balls

Things aren't always good between us, but we still have sex. At least once a day, usually more. He has to fuck all the time; otherwise he gets pissy. I want him to thrive.

The Ex V

I met a few of my friends from high school at Ölsto-fan, a pub downtown, on a cold evening in autumn. It'd been a long time since I'd gone out to meet friends unless it was some big occasion. I've become so socially anxious and shy. He gets jealous when I meet my friends, and I'm afraid I'll give away how crazy I've become, so it's just easier for both of us if I stay at home with him.

There were four of us, and we were in the middle of a conversation when The Ex walked into the pub with a friend. They walked up to the bar, and The Ex spotted me, nodded in my direction as she ordered a beer. Rage flared up inside of me. Why didn't she just fuck off when she saw that I was here with my friends?

There are plenty of bars in Reykjavik; I was here first. I told the girls about the phone call—when The Ex spread the latest gossip she'd heard about me.

My friends all said the same thing—it was a bitch move to make light of the assault. I told them how hurt I was that he hadn't defended me, and then my friend Unnur shot straight up and said, "I'll avenge you." She went up to the bar and ordered a large glass of ice water. I watched anxiously as she crept up behind The Ex, who'd taken a seat at a table near us. Unnur stopped, looked at me. I nodded in approval, and then she slowly poured ice water over The Ex's head, streams of water running down her hair, under her sweater, and down her back. The Ex jumped up and gasped. Unnur sat back down at our table, where we were giggling like idiots. I was so grateful that she'd taken up the sword to defend my honor, and I could feel my gladness all the way down to my Viking DNA.

The Ex stormed over to us. She was dripping wet, her mascara running and smeared. She glared at me. "I did not deserve that," she said. And she stormed back out into the cold night with her friend.

Woman Warrior

I thought he'd be mad about the water incident, but he seemed to feel some sly joy because I'd started a fight over him. He'd already told me how unfortunate he thought it was that I wasn't more competitive. When I told him for the thousandth time that I didn't want to go out with him for a run, he said, "You're really fine, but if you were a bit more of a fighter and bothered to exercise, you'd be a perfect ten."

Up to now, I've never been very interested in competition or sports, and I've never had any need or interest in beating or being better than others. But I'm not going to lose to her, no fucking chance.

Words

He's a master at turning my words against me. He remembers everything better than I do—he just takes the most uncharacteristic things I've said out of context and frames them in an unflattering way. When we fight, he bombards me with my own words. Then I feel like a girl who's cut off her arms and handed them to him in complete trust. Now he's using my own lifeless limbs to hurt me.

Lessons from History

A few days ago he suggested that it might be nice if we started to bake together. The scent of cakes and fresh pastries overpowers the grime, the dust, the sour rags that have saturated the basement apartment. He doesn't know how to bake, and while I work my way through a recipe, he hangs out on the computer in the living room. I have definite doubts about this baking experiment. I'm terrified I'll get fat from eating all this cake. He thinks fat girls are repulsive.

When he was a teenager, he was with a girl for a few years. He was taken with her from the very beginning, but as soon as she started to gain weight, he lost his appetite for her.

Cycle

Sometimes, we boil over. I explode about something or crumble into a pile of self-pity. We bare our teeth, I threaten to leave forever, I sob, he comforts me, we fuck and fall asleep. The next day, we're silent until the world has realigned. Then life goes on, as life always goes on.

Love

He's peeled me like an onion. Surrounded by the leavings of my own sallow skin, I've dwindled to nothing, and my eyes smart.

Contract

One of his friends is doing her master's abroad. She has an apartment on Válastígur, and she's offered to rent it out to him. It's a much better space than the basement apartment, and he's invited me to move in with him ... if I promise to stop acting crazy and cutting myself. Now everything will be better. I tossed out the pocketknife. It's our new beginning.

Household

The new apartment is great! It's right downtown, and we wake up to the bells of Hallgrímskirkja Church. We're close to everything. The kitchen is on the large side and it has these gorgeous orange walls. We stock the fridge with vegetables and health food—no Diet Coke, no hot dogs or meat of any kind. I don't know what'll become of his roommate; I hope he doesn't end up snowed in by piles of dust and lint. We've never had so much room to breathe and be ourselves; we have a living room just for us, plus the bedroom. You could almost go wild from comfort. The living room leads to a beautiful garden. In summer, we can sit there and drink beer and play games. I haven't quite figured out how I'm going to pay my portion of the rent with my gig at the café, but I'm sure it'll turn out okay.

Books

The sheer number of books he has caught me completely off guard. I knew that all the windowsills and empty surfaces in his room were stacked with books, but I had no idea about the rest of them. As we packed everything up, I realized that his closet and all its shelves were full of books instead of clothes. When we ferried over to Válastígur and started to put the books in order, I felt like I was walling myself in. But I've promised to stop being crazy, so I don't breathe a word about the choke of claustrophobia that's encroaching upon me.

Compromise I

Even though we live together now, I don't call him my boyfriend. I think that label is too cliché, and it'd be too awkward after all this time. I call him my fake man.

The Natural Habitat of

Vegetarians

I t's great to feel grown up. On Válastígur, we can have everything the way we want it. We recycle, cook vegetarian meals, read as many books as we want, and sometimes we stay awake all night and watch movies. Our home, on our terms.

Childhood

He has such beautiful eyes. Sometimes he snuggles up to my chest and looks up at me, deep into my soul. Then he's so cute that I almost want to have him, to be his mommy, to start anew and take care of him. He went through so much when he was a kid that can't be taken back. When I asked him to tell me about his life with his father, he drew back, acted strangely, but I know a little bit. I know that his father had all sorts of questionable girlfriends, and some of them were really chaotic, but he usually had time to read in peace when his father was in a relationship. I also know—mainly because of the stories he's told me—that his father was a drunk who didn't tolerate weakness and mistreated his girlfriends.

Like when he was seven years old in Norway, he vomited all over the kitchen table. His father hit him so hard that he knocked him off his chair, and he continued to kick him with steel-toed boots.

Another time, his father took him to some woman's flat and made him wait while he fucked her upstairs. But he got to watch cartoons in the living room. That was a good day to him—until they came home to find his father's girlfriend raving, demanding to know where they'd been.

When he was twelve, he moved back to Iceland. Nobody ever talked about those years in Norway. He wouldn't speak about the alcoholism, the violence. He often tells me that he thinks his mother is clever and beautiful, but on the few occasions he's talked about his father, he's marveled at how his mother could've been with such a jackass.

Primitive

We are naked and sweaty. My ear against his sturdy rib cage, a delicately spicy aroma from his underarms. That is my favorite smell in the entire world. I want to bathe in his sweat, go out into the world with the scent of him ensnaring my senses.

Special Place

Our love is raw. We trust each other down to the core, something nobody in my life has ever come close to. When I feel as if I've flayed myself with a potato peeler, I remind myself: Love is a spectrum. It is as painful as it is wonderful.

Principles

My friend Bryndís is in homemaking school. The other day she came for a short visit to check out the new apartment. She brought a delicious-smelling cake that she'd taken out of the oven just before she came over. He was in his room with his computer the entire time, only saying hello to her when she peeked into the room. When Bryndís had gone, he came out and scrutinized the cake. "What type of eggs did she use?" he asked accusingly. He's much more of a purist than I am. Even though we're both vegetarians, he's much stricter about his diet.

"I don't know, probably just brown eggs," I answered, getting myself a glass of milk to drink with a warm slice of cake.

"Can you call your friend and find out? I'm not going to eat murder eggs."

I did, and Bryndís said that the shells had been white. She apologized, saying they were just the eggs they use in school. I told her it was fine, the cake was surely going to be delicious. He rolled his eyes and grimaced as he watched me try to deal with the egg issue. Just before I hung up, he stormed out of the kitchen and locked himself in the bedroom. He eats only pastries that are baked with brown eggs or eggs from hens that have definitely ranged freely.

I sat alone next to the cake and my glass of milk. I ate the entire fucking cake because I thought it was rude to throw it out. To me, cake is just cake.

Growing Pains

When I visit my parents, he never comes along. Since I've left home, I miss them sometimes. They invite us to dinner all the time, and they're always ready to cook a hearty vegetarian recipe—they never feed us side dishes. It's clear that he's welcome, but he has difficulty being around my folks. My mom and dad are so normal, and he says he doesn't know how he should act.

Sometimes I stay longer than expected, talking or watching a film. Then he gets peeved because he's been sitting at home waiting for me. He doesn't understand why I'm still so attached to my parents. "When are you going to leave the nest? When will *I* get to be your family?"

Treasure Hunt

Often, when I visit people I know, I look in their medicine cabinet. I don't go through it; I just open it and check out its contents, see how it's organized. I've done this since I was little. Back then, I'd rummage through every cabinet in my parents' house in search of treasures, unearthing birthday and Christmas gifts, looking for dark chocolate or spare change to buy myself jellies. The girl who owns the apartment that we're renting took almost all her things with her before she moved out. Except in the kitchen, where she stashed a few things in the lower cabinet.

Ever since we moved in, I've been itching to find out what she left in there. One day, when I was home alone, I emptied out the cabinet—one item at a time. She hadn't left anything really interesting—lots of crockery, crafting supplies, tools. In the toolbox, I found a matchbox, and something inside of it rattled. It was full of wafer-thin paper packages. I picked one out of the box and unfolded it. A stainless steel razor blade. I'd never handled anything like that before; it was featherlike, with an hourglass shape carved out of the middle.

I replaced everything else in the cabinet, carefully putting it all back in its place. Or nearly everything. I took the razor blade that I'd opened and hid it in the bathroom. I haven't cut myself since we moved in, but I think it's good to have the blade on hand, just in case.

Compromise II

When we first met, I was very outspoken. I had principles, feelings about coexistence. People shouldn't piss on the people they care about; they shouldn't sleep around while keeping someone dangling. I thought anal sex was out of the question, I didn't like to give blow jobs, and when I was forthright about all those things, he made a face, like he was gloating. After we started living together, he told me that he knew from the beginning that he would turn me, bring me over to his side.

Depression

A haze in my head. Body fatigued, numb. Housefly lands on my cheek, don't have the energy to swat it away. Eyelids heavy under the weight of air. They fold. I want to sleep for a hundred years. I want to forget myself.

Alchemy

We take turns cooking. But I still do it more often because he's such a messy cook. He splashes food on the walls, fills the sink with pots and pans, the cutting board, dirty utensils. One evening, I'd planned to make a North African stew, and I told him about it the day before; I'd even soaked the beans overnight. But when it came time to cook, I didn't feel like it. I lay in bed all day and didn't want to do anything apart from retreat from the world.

When he found me spread like a jellyfish under the blankets, he lashed out. "You said you were going to cook! I've been looking forward to it all day!" He said that was typical of me; I never do anything I say I'll do, and I never finish anything. I rolled out of bed, shuffled into the kitchen, shutting him out. While I chopped vegetables, I cursed and cried, throwing the ingredients carelessly into the pot. I cooked noisily, tumultuously. I threw the dishes on the table, poured tepid water into a carafe, and called *"Bon appétit!"* when the sweet potatoes were still half hard to the tooth.

In the meantime, he sat at his computer in the living room, not once looking up to acknowledge my cooking conniption. He walked into the kitchen, sat down at the table, grabbed a plate. I watched him scoop a forkful of vegetables and beans, blow on it, and slide it into his mouth. He chewed, scowled, tore off a paper towel, and spat the food back out. Without saying anything, he stood up from the table, grabbed an apple, and went back into the living room, where he sat down in front of his computer.

Knowledge

He is private. I'm not allowed to go through his computer. But I know he's online all the time chatting with other people, other women, and he doesn't want me to have anything to do with it. He works for a nonprofit human rights organization two nights a week, and once, when he was running late for his shift, he forgot his computer as he tore out of the apartment. I was alone at home, and suddenly I realized that the computer, this technology forbidden to me, was left wide open on the coffee table. For a microsecond I thought it would be best to trust him— to leave it alone—but as I sat in front of the computer, I couldn't help but let my eyes wander across the screen.

It was February, dark out. The lights in the living room were off, and the screen's gray-blue gleam shone cold. I saw that he had been talking dirty, flirting with girls while we were together. But the redhead had a special place. He had praised her for her cleverness, her beauty, raved about their encounter, and he regularly made plans to meet her. I read through their messages again and again, calculating them against the amount of time we'd been spending together, like lining up pieces of a puzzle. He had been talking dirty with her while I was baking for him, studying, or on the toilet. He repeated over and over how much he loved her. I realized that, on the first night he told me that he loved me, he'd met up with her at the pub, at Kaffibarinn, told her exactly the same thing, and fucked her. If she hadn't had a boyfriend at the time, he would've almost certainly asked her to move into the apartment on Válastígur.

Disapparation

I am such an idiot. How can one person be this much of a failure? I thought I could just wait it out until I was good enough. That he'd come to love me eventually. But he just looks through me. I am transparent. I don't exist.

Redhead

I lay on the sofa, crying uncontrollably. Trembling under the heavy sobs, my body stiffened into a spasm until I passed out. When I recovered my senses, I felt like I was in a fugue state. I knew. I knew what to do. I went to the bathroom and closed the door behind me. Pulled out the razor blade from its hiding place in the medicine cabinet. Crouched down in the shower, I stuck the blade deep in my left wrist, dragged a determined sluice, pin straight. Everything was in a fog, but I cut again and again, watching as blood sprang from the wound. I smeared the blood into my hair, screamed, cried; I would be a redhead too when he came home. I carved five strokes into the wrist of

my right arm, but they were less substantial, less sure.
I curled up on the floor of the shower and cried until
I lost consciousness.

Capulet

I felt as if I were aboard a submarine, hundreds of meters under the sea. But out of the deep, I heard him close the front door. Damn it, can't I do anything right? I can't even off myself like a proper person. I heard him call me, heard his footsteps as he entered the living room, as he saw the laptop I'd discarded on the floor. I heard him open it, heard the playing of fingers on its keys, the realization that I knew. "Fuck . . . Lilja, where are you?"

I didn't want to answer him. I wanted to lie quiet and still. I wasn't sure if I could talk. My throat was so dry and painful and I was so weak, I didn't believe I could make a sound even if I willed it. I heard him walk through the apartment, search the bedroom, the living room again, the kitchen, and the bath. He knelt beside me, pulled me into his arms, and cried. He lifted my wrist, repeating, "What did you do?" But he's not an idiot; he knew I wasn't dead. He shook me until I moaned an incomprehensible something. I couldn't look him in the face. I had no language for what I had tried to do.

Shame

He wrapped gauze around my arms, dressed me in a big sweater, called a cab. The taxi driver watched me in the rearview mirror the entire time. "She's not going to throw up, is she?"

"No, no, nothing like that," he answered plaintively, reaching for my hand.

In the emergency room, I gave the woman in the window personal details: name, social, address. She asked why I came; I choked. "Do I have to?" I answered quickly. "Can't I just tell the doctor?"

"You have to tell me so that we can assess the urgency of your case."

I looked around. The waiting room was full of people who looked morose, as if they'd been waiting there all evening. I eventually pulled myself together, tempered my thoughts, and said in a half whisper, "I had an accident."

The woman in the glass cage pursed her lips. "What sort of accident?"

I lifted my arm up and showed her the wrinkled bandages, by now seeping blood.

"I understand. Take a seat over there. The doctor will be with you shortly."

We sat on blue vinyl chairs, the arm jabbing my side when I snuggled up to him. He was my shield against the fluorescent lights and the gazes of injured people in the waiting room. "Can't we just go home? I don't want to be here," I whispered.

"You have to let them look at it, then we'll go home," he said, tightening his arms around me.

He'd barely said the words when a young doctor called me. I looked around the room, not quite sure why I was called ahead of everyone else. The doctor led us into an exam room, where I sat on the examination table.

He took a seat in the corner. He looked so stocky, sitting there in the corner and staring at the green laminate floor.

The doctor unwrapped my right arm and said calmly, "Lilja, can you tell me what happened?"

I looked down to avoid his attentive gaze, couldn't answer. Wasn't it obvious? Why did I have to put up with such idiotic questions?

"You have to tell me what happened," he continued slowly.

I started to wail, shaking and shivering, hoping that I wouldn't have to answer any of his questions. The young doctor turned to where he sat in the corner.

"Do you know what happened?"

He raised his hands to his face, wiped aside tears that ran down his cheeks, brushed his lips with the heel of his hand, and began, "I just found her like this. I was at work when she did it."

The young doctor inspected the wounds. Medical staff were constantly coming and going, and he spoke to them in low tones until an older nurse arrived to help. She hung around. She and the doctor whispered to each other before he turned to me, resolved: "Lilja, you have to tell me how you got these wounds."

I was ashamed. Why couldn't I even manage to kill myself? Then I wouldn't have to listen to this bullshit. I couldn't say anything; I had no words to describe what had happened. The doctor pressed me for an answer until I pushed through my silence: "I fell in the shower."

The doc and nurse looked at each other. I expected that they would chide me for lying to them so boldly. But the doctor answered with intention, "What did you hit when you fell? I need to know how you got these wounds in order to assess the severity."

"A razor blade," I answered, ashamed.

He scrutinized the wounds, allowed my answer to suffice, and began to stitch my fissures.

Kindness

I was discharged in the morning with stitches and bandages that itched, that I could not scratch, that I couldn't get wet. Taxis aren't cheap, and we didn't have the money to take a taxi back. As we walked across the hospital parking lot toward the bus stop, we ran into a hippie I recognized from the café where I work. He worked as an emergency nurse, but I hadn't seen him in the bustle of staff that had rushed in and out of my exam room. He said he'd just finished up his shift, and he offered us a ride. I slumped in the back seat like a shameful shit while they made small talk on the way to town. But I've seldom felt as grateful as I did for that ride.

Hibernation

I didn't leave the house for days. A string of days. I didn't answer the telephone, skipped school, asked him to call in sick for me at work. He tried to get me to eat, but my appetite was gone. I felt in a knot in my stomach, worrying that things were over between us. I was too fucked-up, afraid that the contract was broken. But he was gentle, lay with me, held me. Repeated again and again that he loved me so much and he wanted to watch over me. He begged me to keep the suicide attempt from my parents; he was afraid they'd try to keep us apart.

Magma

He dragged me into the living room; we sat there, looking for a movie to watch on his computer. I saw a tab blink. Her name. He was still talking to the redhead. The pressure of anger forced me out of my lethargy. "Are you still talking to that slut? What the hell's wrong with you?" I shoved my bandaged wrists in his face and shrieked, "It's all your fault, you asshole. I hate you!"

He protested, said he'd long ago stopped talking to her, but she kept trying to connect with him. "I only want to be with you. Try to calm down. You can see what she said . . ."

But I had no interest in doing more homework on their chats, nor did I plan on loosening the fist of my righteous anger. I jumped on him, punching and clawing. I throttled him and strangled him and dug my nails into his neck as he begged me to stop and tried to embrace me, but I fought like a wild thing, bit him and struck him, and in the end, he threw me off, and I slammed into the floor, where I lay in a pile and cried until he carried me, my body still furled, into the bedroom.

Mission

My mother called for the hundredth time, and I finally answered. She asked if I was okay, if something was wrong. I feigned illness and said I was on the mend. "I'm happy to hear that," she answered cheerfully. "I'm just in your neighborhood. Did I tell you that your dad and I are getting new curtains? Do you want to come along, check them out?" Mom didn't wait for an answer before adding, "I'll be there in fifteen, be ready."

I tossed the comforter off of me and threw on some clothes, stumbled into the bathroom. I brushed the moss off my teeth, splashed water on my face, tried to freshen my appearance. In the mirror, I saw my sickness, sallowness. Hair in tangles, disordered. I had become so pale that the circles under my eyes were colored black purple. I didn't understand why I had such dark circles; I'd done nothing but sleep for the past few days. I wrapped my hair in a bun and painted over the darkness under my eyes.

Disappointment

"What's this? Do you still have a fever?" Mom asked when I climbed into the passenger seat.

"No, no. I think I'm coming around," I answered, flipping on the radio. It was just past four in the afternoon, but the sun was on its way down. As we inched forward in the traffic, Mom told me about some friend drama with my sister, Gunna. One of the girls had had sex for the first time, and she showed Gunna and the other girls a pair of bloody underpants to prove it.

"They're only twelve—should they be having sex already?" Mom asked, launching back into her story before I had a chance to respond. "Gunna's lost all interest in the piano. We really have to push her to practice at home." My mother talked and talked as we slowly made our way toward the shopping center at Skeifan. I leaned against the cold window, watching a drizzle of sleet fall to the sidewalk, melt into the grayness of the pavement.

Mom parked in front of a pricey furniture store and unstrapped her seat belt. I felt like I couldn't move. I had no way to muster energy for this snob store.

"Come on," Mom said, urging me to unhook my seat belt. I had such a lump in my throat, I couldn't speak. As soon as we made eye contact, I broke into tears. She was completely taken aback. By sheer force of will, I was able to stutter, between deep sobs, "I'm . . . not . . . doing so . . . well . . ."

Mom leaned over the armrest, wrapped her arms around me, tried to comfort me. I felt I didn't deserve how good she was with me, not with how self-centered I'd been. In a calm, almost sedative voice, she asked, "What's wrong, love?"

I couldn't tell her what happened, couldn't talk about it. I had promised to keep the secret, but only halfheartedly. I lifted my arms, turned my wrists toward her.

Mom gasped. And said sadly, "My girl." She tightened her arms around my shaking frame, and we cried together to the murmur of traffic in the parking lot.

The Situation

I'm not going to leave him. I don't want to go home to Mom and Dad. *He* takes care of me now.

Out and About

My mom made me an appointment with a psychiatrist. His office is right in the mall. When she told me about it, I quipped that it was very convenient that the shopping center offered its patrons both manic consumption and the psychological help to cure it, but she didn't get the joke. He came with me to the office. As we walked the polished tiles of this temple of Mammon, concern that we'd run into the redhead crept up on me. Maybe she'd see us together and assume that I still didn't know about them, that I was just this unsuspecting idiot girl who really believed she had a good boyfriend.

Appointment I

The psychiatrist lifted a gigantic notepad and, as I spoke, scribbled notes here and there on the blank pages. I told him that I'd tried to off myself. That the man I loved was a womanizer, but things had gotten better. I answered his questions as honestly as I could: Yes, I cry often. No, I don't go out of the house much. No, I haven't thought about doing it again. The doctor called me *dear* and *sweetie*—I hate it when strange men do that, but I didn't mention it. I'm polite.

As the appointment went on, I asked the psychiatrist questions that I hadn't dared ask another person, but he's a professional, so he can't disclose any of the nagging worries that I air in his office: "Can I stay with him, even though he's cheated on me?"

The psychiatrist took a long pause, laced his sausage fingers together under his chin, and said thoughtfully, "Breaches of trust are remarkably common in relationships. There are a number of ways to work through issues like this. You have a choice: Do you want to try to forgive him and stay together? If you don't believe you can do that, the only option is to end the relationship."

"But I want to stay together," I answered, relieved.

At the end of the appointment he wrote a prescription that he wanted me to begin taking immediately.

Ground Zero

The pills flatten me, make me into a thin scum on the surface of still water. I don't sink. Coast instead, detached from the world around me, and I'm fine with it. Time is water, and the weeks run like a current beneath me, without me.

Appointment II

The psychiatrist comments that I'm losing weight, asks if my appetite has decreased. I shrug. "Maybe. I don't really know," I answer.

That's a fringe benefit of this medication. I don't want to eat. I am finally thin.

Desire

I have no desire for anything—not food, not entertainment, not sex. But we still sleep together. For him, sex is a clear measure of how happy relationships are. The beginning of the end is usually when people stop having sex. We sleep together a lot, multiple times a day.

Sex has become a chore, like doing the dishes; you have to stay on top of it so that the mess doesn't get out of control. I haven't told him about the horror of feeling nothing. I don't want him to believe he's bad in bed. He's not bad. The sex has gotten rough. I just want him to take control, to shake me out of this deadness. He slaps my ass, digs his nails into my skin, pulls my hair when he fucks me from behind. If he looks into my eyes while we're fucking, I tell him to grab my neck, to choke me, and sometimes I hope he'll lose control in the heat of the moment and kill me. But accidentally, so that he feels bad and has to call my parents crying and beg their forgiveness for riding their daughter to death. That would be good of him.

Cold Slab

Night after night, I have the same nightmare: I'm having cocktails, and I'm surrounded by attractive, well-to-do people. The scene glitters with light refracting off crystal champagne flutes and necklaces clasped around women's necks. Frivolous laughter. The clinking of glasses. In the middle of the room, under an enormous crystal chandelier, there's an elegant buffet set with exotic fruits, berries, and colorful canapés. In the middle of the table lies a thin girl, stripped of her clothes. She's awake, staring straight ahead, sublimely detached. Before her, a row of carefully laid knives, sharpened to a sure point, not unlike the sterile scalpels of surgical carts. A grand middle-aged woman in an emerald dress that drags on the floor taps a spoon on her glass, announcing that it's time to dig in. They line up one after another, slicing into the wafer-thin skin, binging on the pale morsels of her body. I go up to the girl, prod her with a knife, but she doesn't react. I slice striploin from her skinny frame, relishing the cold, salty meat.

As the room empties out, the woman in the green gown is beside herself because there's so much food left over. She asks me to take the remains of the meal home.

I follow the woman into the kitchen. The girl is standing there, ghostly pale, wrapped in plastic. I throw her over my shoulder like a sack of potatoes, carry her to my car. But it feels too cruel to put her in the trunk, so I place her in the passenger seat. When I put the car in gear, she begins to tremble violently, as if she's just come alive, and she begins to breathe quickly, erratically. I take her home, wrap a blanket around her, and talk to her. She doesn't seem to comprehend anything. She shakes, consumed by choked breaths. I can't save her. I can't ease her suffering. I am complicit. I know she won't linger much longer. I try to offer her food. I try to do something good for her, but I know the time for salvation has passed.

Resolution

I have been working very hard to forgive him. I will, with time. He's so beautiful, it'd be difficult not to offer him forgiveness. I find it much more difficult to forgive myself for being such a psychotic idiot. For not having known better, for not having left, for letting it carry on so long.

Balance

I 've always tried to be a good person, and I'm pretty sure I used to be. But these days I have nothing to give, nothing to say. I'm here, but I'm completely lost. My parents taught me that patience, empathy, and hard work were key to a happy life. If I treated people with kindness, everything would turn out fine. But now I find that I've become emotionally bankrupt, having given away much more than I ever had to begin with.

Untoward Effects

Nothing has improved. The meds are a bandage on a gash. With the least provocation, my fissures open up, blood and pus erupt from the wound, and the only remedy is more medicine so that I don't feel as much. I go easy on myself; I take pains, I wrap myself in cotton. I never meet anybody or make plans. I don't force myself to move. At first the pills dried up the well of my tears, but now the tears have welled over. I grieve for us and the relationship that I believed we would have.

Sleeping Beauty

I had an appointment with my GP at eleven o'clock on Tuesday morning to refill my contraceptives. I set the alarm clock, but when it went off, I didn't get up. I couldn't wake up. I couldn't move. I meant to press snooze but turned it off instead. I slept until two in the afternoon, and I didn't wake up when the doctor's office called—twice. I wasted their time. I can't show my face there again. I'll just find another way to take care of the pills. I'll just wait until I meet the psychiatrist again—he seems eager enough to scribble down scripts for whatever I want.

Optimism

I finished my birth control pills a week ago. It was no problem getting a new prescription from my psychiatrist. The new pills are already in our bathroom cabinet. The doc said I had to wait for my next period before I can start taking them. I'm not worried about this break—in fact I've suspected for years that I might be infertile. When I was fucking around, I was often reckless, and nothing ever happened.

He hates condoms, says they're uncomfortable and unnatural. I'm pretty sure he's never had to use them with other girls. We haven't ever, at least. I don't mind him cumming in me.

Drought

I've always been irregular. Maybe I've become anemic. Maybe it's the meds. Maybe I'm like a Russian ballerina who's starved off her womanhood. I'm not squeamish about blood; let it overflow the banks, flood between my thighs, through my pants.

Absence

I've kept quiet over the fact that he has two children for so long that their existence has become a massive lie. I don't think my parents would mind him being a father—that's just how life goes sometimes. But I'm pretty sure they would have reservations about him not taking care of them. He's never visited his kids while we've been together, probably because it's hard enough as it is to have to look after his crazy girlfriend.

Going Down

Our bed is descending slowly into the ground, like an elevator. I touch the cold, wet walls of earth. The darkness becomes thicker, but if I concentrate and stare straight upward, I see in the distance our bedroom ceiling. The bed sinks deeper and deeper, I have no control over this mechanism. There are no buttons, no way to get back up. Dirt and insects slowly fall on my mattress, filling it up. In the muck, I roll over to my other side and try to sleep some more.

Situation

I don't think there's any reason to take the pregnancy test seriously. He says that if I'm really pregnant, I have to keep the baby; it was created in love. He says he'll help me as little or as much as I want. I don't know what to believe; he never thinks about his other kids, but he says this time it'll be different.

Appointment III

"Has the crying increased?" the psychiatrist asked.

"Ya, I think so," I answered, drying my eyes with my sleeve.

"And how is it going with him?" he asked, leaning back in his chair.

I straightened up, swallowed the lump in my throat, and mustered as much dignity as I could. "It's going well, thanks."

The psychiatrist *hmmed* and *I see'd*, and said finally, "Well, it's not good that your mood swings haven't evened out, my dear. We can add another medication to try to stabilize you." He turned to his computer and entered a new prescription as he continued to mumble toward his keyboard about the mechanism of action and the purpose of the medication.

I interrupted. "Listen, I was thinking about . . . well . . . I think I might be pregnant—would that be a problem?"

The doctor looked up from the keyboard, screwing up his eyes, as if contemplating something.

"Why do you think that?" he asked.

"I took a pregnancy test yesterday that showed—well. I don't know, maybe it's just a false positive."

The psychiatrist picked up his phone and punched in an extension. "Hello. I've got a patient here that I would like you to look at . . . yes, exactly, thank you." He set down the receiver, rose to his feet, and directed me to follow him. We went into the next room and met with an OB/GYN, obviously a close colleague of his. They talked about my potential pregnancy as if I weren't there. "Patient reports she took a pregnancy test that returned a positive result. I need to confirm before I can prescribe her Diazepam."

The gynecologist, a lively older man, answered lightly, "Let's take a look. I'm available till three."

Crossroads

There's no room for another person in our relationship; we are already enough to handle. We can't have a child together. We can hardly be together. It won't be long now until I dissolve, disappear, become nothing. I don't know what's best. I've strayed too far from myself to think right. But I know that my choice is between having him and having the baby, between staying together and severing myself from our root system. To me, it's one or the other. A termination, no matter what I do.

Afterlife

Naked from the waist down on the examination table, I was suddenly self-conscious about how long it'd been since I shaved my legs. I hadn't noticed how hairy they'd gotten until I saw them propped up in front of me. The gynecologist asked me to scoot to the edge of the table. "Now, here comes something cold," he said as he slid in a metal instrument to spread my vagina. Next, he slipped what looked like a large condom onto a plastic baton that he eased into me. He studied the screen, moved the instrument at different angles, searching. "There we go!" he said. "There it is." He turned the screen toward me. "See, there—there's a little heart beating inside you."

Cosmogenesis

On a dark screen I see a little light blinking rapidly.

Second heart: my way out.

    Little heart, thrive, grow, and beat in time with mine.

You are my light out of this darkness.